CONDEMNED TO THE HUCOW PRISON

Steamy Milking Story

Leandra Camilli

CONTENTS

CHAPTER 1

"The way I see it, Princess, this is your only option," the lawyer sitting across the desk told me. The way Charles was looking at me, it was obvious that he was genuine about his words. My only option. To go to the Hucow Prison, where I didn't know how much my life was going to change. And I was already thinking about it that way, with that level of certainty, mostly because I knew I was going to go there and take that route.

I let out a cloud of breath, feeling it moving over my breasts. There was no denying that they were round and big, something that was already making the lawyer steal glances down at them whenever he could.

And given that I kept on looking down pretty much all the time, feeling so completely ashamed of myself, he had many opportunities to do that.

"I still don't like it."

Charles put the papers down on the desk. Even though he wore a dark suit and it hid most of his body, there was no denying that he was a sight for sore eyes. The stubble on his face, his nose, his plump lips, the harsh cheekbones, and pretty much everything else were making me feel a little hint of lust in me. I couldn't help but wonder what he was like when he was naked after taking a shower.

I imagined Charles walking out of his bathroom with only a towel covering his body. Or maybe he lived alone and he would step out of the bathroom without even that covering him. The thought alone was enough to make me feel slightly wet, and I suddenly found myself rubbing my legs together.

"You don't have to like it, but there is something I can do to make your time there less hard on you," he proposed and I lifted my eyes up. I was still looking down at my legs before that, but now that he was giving me some hope, I wanted to know everything about it.

I noticed him letting out a shadow of breath, his eyes studying me and sizing me up.

And... It was such a pity that I was finally noticing that he had a marriage ring on his finger. I didn't know he was taken, and it was already making me shake my head in complete disappointment.

The worst thing was remembering that I was still a virgin and that I didn't think that that was going to change anytime soon.

"What is it that I can do?" I asked and Charles stood up slowly. I watched carefully as he did that. There was something about the way he moved his body, how tall he was, the shape of his muscles, his confident posture, and pretty much everything else that made me want him completely.

"I'm not sure I should say it." Charles took another deep breath and then stepped over to the window. It overlooked a huge, impressive garden, and even though I was in love with it when I first came here, I didn't have enough time to study it. I wanted to explore it, to feel what it was like to be with those bushes and small trees, but I had something much more important to do here. Not to mention that I was pretty sure the police would not have let me go there, in the first place, without making a fuss about it, and I didn't want to go through that hassle.

I was checking his behind carefully and slowly. Since stepping into his office, it was the first time that I was having this opportunity. And Charles didn't stop before putting his hand inside his pocket and lighting up a cigarette. Even though I didn't like the smell of the smoke, the fact that he was smoking was making him look even more appetizing than before. I was trying to control it, but it was impossible. My mouth was salivating. I could feel the slow buildup of saliva in it.

I stood up slowly as well. I felt like I needed to be closer to that man as much as possible. Not to mention that I had this strong urge to rip the clothes off his body, and something about the way he was talking right now was telling me that he just might be thinking the same.

I mean, even though Charles was married, there was no denying that he found me incredibly hot. And that thought alone was enough to make me feel waves of lust in my body. They were hardening my nipples, and that was something that didn't happen often. After all, where I lived, I didn't see guys as hot as he was.

"I want to know what it is. I want to know everything," I said and he finally turned around. He took a drag off his cigarette and then he blew some smoke out of his mouth and into my face. I cringed, but I didn't complain about what he just did. The smell of the smoke was truly horrible, though. It was churning my stomach.

I took a deep breath and then said, "There's no point in dancing around the truth. I know you want me. You keep looking at me a little funny, your eyes keep going down and looking at my crotch, and I know that you noticed I was doing the same with your breasts. They are amazing. Incredibly plump, big, round, and they look so heavy, too. I can't help but wonder what it would be like to have my hands all over them. But right now, I am thinking about doing something else."

My heart was speeding up. I knew Charles was a perceptive man, but I never thought he was so bold.

"I suppose there's no point in denying the truth," I said and he smiled evilly. His hands went for the buckle of his belt, he took it off, and then his pants fell down to the floor. And what my eyes were now seeing was out of this world.

I knew he had a massive, incredibly heavy bulge, but I didn't think that, when he was without his pants, it was going to look so inviting and lust-inducing.

I was already falling to my knees and I knew that I was going to give him an incredible, amazing blowjob that he would never

LEANDRA CAMILLI

forget.

CHAPTER 2

But that all happened in the past. I was at the prison now and the man that was in front of me was holding a small notebook in his hands. He was taking notes about me. I was fully naked and he kept on walking around me slowly and carefully. I could see his eyes moving up and down.

There was something about my body that Carl could see and I didn't know what it was. All I knew was that the fact he was sizing me up like this was making me feel tingles of excitement through my body.

When I was in the lawyer's office, I didn't hold back before giving him a blowjob he would never forget. Charles even told me that it was much better than the last time his wife did the same for him. He also said that it was a pity that I was going to the Hucow Prison.

I was going to be transformed here. They were going to turn me into a hucow and all the milk that I was going to be producing was going to go to the supermarkets across the country. Even though my fate wasn't exactly great, it was much better than dying. That was my other option. The lawyer didn't exactly mention it during the short meeting I had with him, but I already knew about it.

After all, I killed someone and that was something that would never be forgotten or forgiven.

Such was the law in the country. And yet, something about what was happening right now in my life was actually making me feel comfortable about it. I wasn't going to hide it. I was a slut and that would never change. So much so that the guy that was walking around me didn't hesitate before saying, "You look nothing short of stunning, and your transformation will be a smooth and uncomplicated one. Not much about your body will change, Mrs. Hurt."

I didn't know how to take that. I thought that my transformation was going to change me completely. I was even already imagining myself with wider curves, bigger breasts, and a much rounder ass - something that would make the bulls in this facility lust after me.

"Should I feel good about that?" I asked and he finally stopped in front of me. He put down the small notebook he was holding and then he stepped over to me. Carl was so close to me that I could feel the strong, unbelievable smell of his cologne, and it was intoxicating my lungs.

"I think you should," he said and when he lifted his hand and put it on my shoulder, I didn't flinch or try to move away from him. After all, there was something about his hand that was turning me on even more than I already was.

After a moment of silence, he asked, "You are enjoying this, aren't you, Mary? This isn't the first time you are alone with a man." And his affirmation was spot on. So much so that when he lowered his hand so that he was feeling my arm, cherishing the smoothness and softness of my skin, I didn't try to stop him, even though there were clear rules about inmate and guard relationships. He was more than a guard, but that was beside the point.

The point was that I was looking at this as an opportunity to get some benefit so that my life at the prison was better.

And thus, I didn't hesitate before sagging to my knees. Carl's fingers were already working on his belt and then he finally took it off. His pants didn't immediately fall down to the floor, but I quickly fixed that. I lowered his pants and then I could finally see the big, massive bulge that was in front of my eyes, and I noticed that I was at the perfect height so that I could suck him off gently. My back wasn't even going to hurt.

"Gosh, you are so stunning it's a pity that you have to live here. I wish I could take you to live elsewhere, maybe even in my house," he murmured, and then I put my fingers under his pair of boxer briefs. It was dark and it contrasted nicely with the peachy color of his skin.

And after I finally lowered his pants and his dong was bouncing up and down and pointing at me, I noticed that my mouth was already drooling. I brushed the back of my hand on both sides of my mouth so that I fixed that, and then I looked up so that I had his permission.

And Carl didn't hesitate before nodding slowly and once. He was giving me what I was looking for, and as someone that was going to give my second blowjob in my life, I was feeling a little anxious. I had some experience after that meeting with the lawyer, but I knew that I had to pull something different this time so that the prison guard had an amazing orgasm. And given the look on his face, there was no denying that he thought I was going to pull it off.

It was with that thought in mind that I put my fingers around his prick, lowering his skin slowly and nicely. My eyes studied how his cockhead looked. It was slightly spongy, pre-cum was leaking out through the slit, and it was also mushroom-shaped.

I didn't know what it was about this prison, but something about it was telling me that it was the perfect place for someone like me, who was always feeling so slutty and horny all the time.

CHAPTER 3

Giving his dick a couple of strokes, the smile on his face was all the confirmation I needed. I could feel the air in the room swirling around me and even though it was a little cold, the heat pulsing out of Carl's body was warming it.

If my life in this prison was going to be like this for the foreseeable future, then I could imagine myself living greatly here and without complaining about anything.

"That's it, Mary. You can do anything and everything. Just make sure that you are doing it well," he ordered and I knew that he was expecting a lot from me. I didn't know if I could deliver it, but I was going to do my best.

I took a deep breath in and when I noticed that he was fully hard, I lowered my head until my lips were around his massive prick. He was incredibly big and I could feel his mushroom-shaped cockhead spreading my lips wide. They were already so stretched wide that I was fearful that they would never return to normal.

Breathing was becoming difficult, but the pleasure that was flowing in ripples in my body was incredibly addictive, too.

I focused on rubbing my tongue on the underside of his dickhead. Carl wasn't ruthless and he wasn't grabbing my hair yet so that he could dictate the pace he wanted. And I was pretty sure that if he was to do that, he wouldn't be merciful with me.

In the meantime, I could keep on sucking him off, following my own pace. I noticed that he was moaning gently and slightly, which meant that he was enjoying this. That, in turn, was giving me more confidence, and I was brushing my tongue over his cock without even wondering when this would finally end.

"Holy shit, you are so fucking good," he murmured and I could feel his fingers moving over my head. He was tempting me. He was showing me that he was going to grab my hair soon if I didn't make him come in the next couple of minutes, and he didn't need to worry about that.

I was actually going to do that right at this moment.

It was with that thought in mind that I increased my pace. I was bobbing up and down on his rock-hard, veiny cock, and I was enjoying every minute of this. It was 'every minute' because it was already a couple of minutes since I started to work on his cockhead, and I never thought it was going to last so long.

I could feel his pre-come smearing my tongue and I was tasting it without showing a hint of shame. It was as I said before. I was a slut and that was not going to change. I could already imagine myself becoming his plaything for the rest of my stay here – and given the sentence they gave me, that was going to be my entire life.

I noticed that his balls were so big and plump, and I couldn't contain myself before grabbing them with my hand. But even then, I felt like one hand wasn't enough. I needed to use both of my hands so that I could worship his balls the way it was supposed to be.

He threw his head backward and shut his eyes. I knew that Carl was feeling immense pleasure from this, which meant that we were going to do this many more times in the future. I did make sure to check out his hand and he didn't have a marriage ring on it.

Carl did have some rings on his fingers, but none of them was a marital one, which already brought a smile to my face even as I continued to thrust my head up and down on his manhood.

Seconds later, I felt him throbbing in my mouth and it was the most delicious and rewarding sensation I had in quite a long time. So much so that I didn't stop myself before thrusting my hand down and then finding my clit. When my finger was touching it, I started to rub it slowly before I picked up the pace. I knew I was going to come and it was going to be so exhausting that I was probably going to pass out.

I didn't hold back before I ran my lips across his massive dick and then I gave it a little peck of good luck. Moments later, Carl started to unload his plentiful load all over my face, and it was hot and creamy, and also sticky. My fingers desperately tried to get as much of his cum as they could, and then I was licking them off with my tongue.

I knew I was looking like the sluttiest woman in the world and I wasn't ashamed of that.

After what felt like minutes later, Carl finally put his prick back under his pants. I was a little sad that our little sexy time was over, but there was nothing I could do about it. All I knew was that it was amazing and that I would certainly ask for more of this when the time was right.

But now that he was picking up his notebook again, I knew that he had something else he wanted to tell me.

Carl sighed and I didn't like the look on his face. If he had something troubling to tell me, then he needed to do that right now.

My body was still feeling the aftershocks of our sex. I noticed that the room was reeking of it, and even though it was supposed to be a little nasty, I was okay with it.

"It shames me to say this, but I'm not the only one that can have you," he stated and I knew he was telling me the truth.

I had no idea what was going to happen now, but I was aware that it was going to shake me to the core.

CHAPTER 4

Carl settled his hand on my shoulder and then he started to lead me out of there and he took me somewhere else in the prison. We crossed several hallways before we finally reached a door where he stopped with me.

Carl was wrapping his fingers around the doorknob as his eyes locked with me again. "Whatever happens here, you have to promise me you won't try to stop it. I know it might hurt, but it's going to be the best thing that ever happened in your life."

I didn't know what it was he was talking about, but after sucking him off and getting to him properly, I knew I could trust him.

And after thinking that, I nodded. Carl opened the door and then I found myself in a much different, darker room. After stepping inside, I noticed I couldn't see much of what was in the room. A light hung from the ceiling and it made a peculiar machine there slightly visible.

I couldn't fully describe it. The machine was different, and yet it still felt like it was calling me to it. Without even thinking about what I was doing, I started to pad toward it. I vaguely remembered I was still naked and that Carl was following me from behind. Even though he just had his climax with me and it was memorable, I knew that he wanted more of that and that he was enjoying the view in front of him, even though he couldn't see much.

"That's the milking machine," he murmured behind me, and then I felt his hand moving down on my body. I didn't stop him or whirl around as if I thought he was doing something despicable. In fact, it was the opposite. I cherished feeling his hand slithering over the curves of my back.

When his hand was on my ass, he gave it a little squeeze. It wasn't too strong, but it was enough to propel me forward. I then found myself no more than a couple of inches from what he called the milking machine.

I put my hand on it and it was slightly cold to the touch. I noticed that Carl stepped over to the other side of the room and then his finger flipped up a switch, and light bulbs that were hanging from the ceiling inundated the room with their glow.

Finally, I could see everything that was happening here. This was almost more like a science facility. Even though nobody told me anything about this, I was certain that they ran several tests here. I was going to be one of their test subjects. I was supposed to be angry at that, but I felt the opposite.

Carl came over to me and he put down his notebook again. A small table stood by one of the sides of the machine.

"Lie down on it. You're going to enjoy this," Carl said and I couldn't say no. After all, he asked that I didn't try to stop what was going to ensue here. I took a deep breath, lied down on the machine, and then he attached two suction tubes, one for each of my breasts.

They were slightly cold, but nothing that turned me off or anything like that. I noticed that a small mound was positioned against my pussy, and I couldn't help but start rubbing against it gently.

Seeing that, Carl started to chuckle slightly, and I had to shoot my head up and ask, "What are you finding so funny?"

He slid his hand over my backside again. It was like he was looking at me as his trophy, and I was certainly enjoying that.

"No, it's just that every new candidate that comes here finds that little mound over there and they instantly fall in love with it."

Well, I was certainly enjoying it and thus I didn't stop myself, rubbing my pussy against it over and over. My body was getting hotter and I couldn't stop myself. It was so good to be rubbing my flower against the mound, and there was nothing to stop me from continuing to do that anyway.

Seconds later, when I felt like minutes passed, I was finally cumming. My body was shaking slightly, and it was one of the most indescribable feelings in all of my life.

When I stopped, I looked up and I noticed that Carl was looking at me with wide eyes. He couldn't believe what just happened.

"You came so quickly that it's incredible that it took you so long when we were fucking," he murmured and I knew he was right to be surprised by it. I never thought I was going to reach my climax so soon after I started to rub my cunt over the little mound on the bed part of the machine.

He then got on his knees slowly and carefully. There was a big, red button on the side of the mechanism and he pressed it. The moment he did that, the machine started to whir. It was shaking and rumbling slightly underneath me, and then I felt the suction tubes applying pressure on my boobs.

As they did that, something was injected into me. I didn't know what it was, but upon looking behind my shoulder, I realized that it was a small syringe.

There was this machine arm, and it was used to apply whatever substance was in it. When it was done doing that, it moved away. I watched it as it retracted behind the backside of the machine. It was almost like what just happened didn't.

Carl was petting my forehead as he said, "Your transformation finally started, and you are going to be changed dramatically. It's not going to be like it always happens with the other girls, but you are still going to look amazing, especially with this round rump that you have over here."

He gave it a little squeeze again, and as the seconds passed, I passed out.

I knew that when I woke up again, I was going to find something that was going to shake me to the core, just like this recent revelation.

CHAPTER 5

When I woke up, there was this hand playing with my fingers and I noticed that a man was standing in front of me. Looking up, I began to realize that he was someone I knew.

Charles Cosenza, the lawyer I met and whose cock I sucked.

He was with his hand around his prick and it was massive – as massive as the other time I was with him.

"Good morning, sweetheart. I hope you slept well," he said and the tone of his voice said everything about what he was thinking right now. He was finding this situation so funny, and also incredibly hot and sexy.

"What's going on?" I asked as I realized that the machine where I was lying was still pumping my boobs, and now I noticed that milk was spurting out into the suction tubes. Turning my eyes to the right, I noticed that it was all going to some huge, impressively big storage barrels.

They were going to sell my milk, and that realization was enough to get me going. And without even thinking about it, as if it was something that happened naturally, I began to scrub my pussy against the little mound that was on the bed attached to the machine.

"It's your first milking, hucow," he said and the fact that he called me that told me everything about what my life was going to be like here from now on. This prison was going to be much more than just that.

"Can I... Milk something else?" I asked, winking. My eyes went down slowly and I examined his massive, oversized manhood. It was so incredibly big, so veiny, and so thick that I couldn't stop staring at it.

"What is it that you want to milk?" He asked, murmuring as he brushed his hand over my cheek. It was remarkably calloused and I wanted to be sucking on his fingers. It was like Charles read my mind and then he put two of his fingers inside my mouth.

And I started to suck on them gently and carefully.

Minutes later, when I was still rubbing my cunt against the mound on the bed and the machine was still working as it continued to milk me, he pulled his fingers back. I was a little disappointed, but it wasn't at all surprising. After all, when I asked him if I could suck something else, I was talking about his slab of meat.

My eyes couldn't stop looking at the pre-come that was seeping through the slit.

"You want this more than anything, don't you?" He asked and I nodded. He smiled evilly and then he took another step toward me. Now, his cock was already touching my lips and I couldn't help myself. I thrust my head forward slightly and then I enveloped my lips around his mushroom-shaped cockhead. It was warm and incredibly wet. The pre-cum that was leaking through the slit was also another delight, and I couldn't stop moving my tongue around his gland, getting as much of that as I could.

And while I was doing that, Charles tilted his head back slightly and then started to moan gently. His moans filled the room and I didn't realize that the backside of the machine was moving. It was opening up and I just noticed that someone was stepping closer from behind me.

I felt him putting his hands on my legs and then he started to glide them up, finally finding the crack of my ass. He drove a finger between my ass crack and then he started to play with my orifice, his finger making circular motions.

"Absolutely amazing. You are so hot and tight," he murmured and then he took another step so that he was right where my orifice was, and I could feel his prick nudging there. It didn't take long for him to ease it in, one inch at a time, and then he was all the way inside of me.

I didn't look behind my way back, but I knew that he was none other than Carl. I was being fucked by two men at the same time and it was the most exhilarating, satisfying thing that ever happened in my life. It was so much better than the two blowjobs that I gave.

I was still sucking off Charles when Carl started to piston in and out of me, his balls slapping against my ass.

He was utterly dominating while doing that, and that coupled with the blowjob that I was giving to Charles and the fact that Carl was ramming it in and out of me without showing any mercy were enough to make me orgasm. And I did that with pleasure. My body then rocked, shaking uncontrollably and I couldn't stop it. Not even if I wanted to.

And when it was over, I was huffing and gasping for air.

And even that wasn't enough. Without warning me, Charles pressed a different button on the side of the machine, and then I was taken off it. He grabbed me in his arms and then he put one of my nipples inside his mouth. My milk was leaking and spraying everywhere as if my body still thought the suction tubes were still sucking on them.

"Jesus fuck, I want this milk so fucking badly," he murmured as he started to suckle on that boob, and then on the other one for good measure.

Carl looked so jealous it was funny. So much so that he didn't hold back before snatching me off his competitor's arms and then doing the same that he was doing before.

I just finished feeding them my milk, and it was the most satisfying thing that ever happened in my life. I was even with a huge, victorious smile on my face when it was finally over.

EPILOGUE

I was in my cell and I wasn't going to go anywhere. My hands were gripping the bars in front of me and I was trying to look at what was at the end of the hallway between the cells. I thought I heard his voice before, but it appeared that I was only imagining things. I was still where I was before – The Hucow Prison.

I supposed it was a good thing that they were keeping me in a separate cell. I noticed that the cell bars were slightly cold and thus I pulled my hands back. I was turning around slowly when I heard footsteps coming from the entrance of the hallway.

And then I heard him whistling gently and slowly. Other than his whistling, everything around me was quiet and serene.

That had to be Carl. He was the one that took the virginity of my asshole, and I was hoping he was coming here to finish the job. Seconds later, which felt more like minutes, he was finally standing in front of the cell where I was.

He was looking at me with mocking, evil eyes. I wondered if he was going to do what I wanted, and then he responded to me by putting his hand in his pocket, and then he took out his keys. He chose one, opened the door of the cell, and then stepped inside.

His fingers were already unbuckling his belt and then he let his pants fall down to the floor. He was as hung as before, and pre-come was already seeping through the little slit of his mushroom-shaped cockhead.

"I know you want this. You are still lactating, right?" He asked as he murmured and given how horny I was right now, I couldn't stop myself before I went down on my knees on the floor, and then I turned around gently so that he was seeing my ass.

Carl was checking it out gently and slowly before he said, "Jesus, you are still so delicious."

The prison guard didn't say anything else as he stepped around me and then he went down on his knees. He positioned himself underneath me and then he grabbed one of my udders. That's what they were called now. They were much more than my breasts. They were always filled with milk and Carl and Charles absolutely enjoyed that.

"Let me have a little taste," he murmured as he put my nipple inside his mouth, and then he started to suckle on it gently, his tongue more often than not moving rapidly around the swollen nub.

That was enough to get me going. My body was starting to get hot, breathing was beginning to get difficult, and my eyes were starting to roll inside my head. Not much longer after that, I was already reaching the peak of my climax. It was hot and unforgiving, something that made Carl open a devilish smile even as he continued to chug more and more of my milk.

A moment later, he moved away from me and then stepped around me slowly. He was stroking his prick as he went down on his knees again. My legs were trembling slightly, but I knew that I could continue being in this position for as long as he needed.

And then, without giving a warning, Carl grabbed me by the waist and nudged the entrance of my pussy with his oversized prick. He was with his body over mine and he wasn't ashamed as he started to ease his dong inside of me.

I couldn't help but wonder one thing and, upon thinking that, I asked him, "Where's Charles?"

"Do you really want to know that?" He asked back and then he began to move his dick further inside of me. When he met the first resistance against it, he made no fuss about it before he thrust forward without showing a hint of shame about it.

He just popped my hymen, and it was such an indescribable feeling. I wasn't a virgin anymore, and that was something I was going to hang around my neck when I had the opportunity to do that, and I could ask him to put a sign there so that everyone knew he was the one that stole my V-card.

"You are so incredibly tight and warm," he murmured into my ear as he started to roll his hips. His pace was slow in the beginning as he started to get used to the size, shape, and everything else that defined my core.

When he was finally used to all of those things, he picked up the pace. I could feel his balls slapping against my ass cheeks and it was so incredible that I began to match him thrust for thrust. With his finger rubbing and worshiping my little bundle of nerves, I came one more time, and this time he held me close to him – almost as if he was fearing that I was going to escape from him or do something just as absurd.

Carl cummed with me, his hot jets filling my tunnel, and then he only pulled out when he was finally done. As he stood up slowly, I noticed that his rod was slightly dirty, something that I couldn't look at without feeling a huge urge in me. And that urge could only be satiated by cleaning him until it was looking pristine and the faint light in the cell was shining off the skin of his manhood.

"You want this, don't you?" He asked and I nodded.

He gave me the permission I needed to clean him up, I did that, and I contemplated what my life was going to be like here for the rest of it.

Charles and Carl, two hung men fucking me and ravaging my pussy without showing a hint of shame about it.

It couldn't be better.

The End

Looking for similar books? Don't forget to check the next page, then.

And leave a review if you liked this story. It really helps me.

TEASER: COWBOYS' HOLIDAY AGE GAP

Fertile First Time Bundle

Perhaps everything would be so much easier if that hunk of a man wasn't seated across from me. We were in the dining room, and I wasn't alone.

His colleague was also with us, picking up a glass of wine and taking a sip from it. His eyes were locked with mine and it was like he was trying to read my mind.

I wasn't trying to read his mind, but I was ogling him without making it obvious I was doing that. I had no idea if he was picking that up, but he smiled and I could see the beautifulness of his super white teeth.

I was just checking him out, wishing I could be in his arms. They looked so strong, confident, veins popping out where I could more easily see them, hair in all the right places, and his skin tanned by the light of the sun. I'd been fantasizing about him since coming here.

And it wasn't just Walter's arms that made my pussy wet, but also his face. And more specifically, his lips.

I wouldn't say that they were big, but they look just right and I knew that if I were kissing them now, I'd be tasting how sweet they were.

His face was chiseled and looked perfect. He groomed his full, thick beard every day, and it looked sharp without making him look gay.

It gave him that extra spice of manliness I always craved in a man. Looking down slightly, I also loved how his beard transitioned to his neck. I could just imagine myself lying in his bed with him and cradling my head in the crook of his neck. I was pretty sure he would love it if I did that.

But something was impeding me from doing that, and it was the fact that I was a virgin. I didn't know much about these two guys, but I knew that they craved women that had a lot more experience.

I didn't want to disappoint them or myself.

His blond hair seemed to draw my attention to him, and I couldn't control that I was ogling it too. It was short, a bit bigger at the top, and even shorter at the sides. I had no idea if he got his hair cut often, but it was always sharp. This wasn't the first time I was checking him out, after all.

His eyes were icy blue and I suddenly found myself entranced by them. His eyes showed me that behind his tough persona, he was a free-spirited and extroverted man. I didn't need that to tell me that was what he was like, but it was great having that confirmation again.

Seated beside him was his colleague. He was forking a piece of meat on his plate, and I noticed the veins popping out on his forearms. His skin was also white, but just as tanned.

He didn't have a full beard like Walter, but his stubble actually made him look sexier. I could just imagine what it would be like to be grazing my hands over his chin and jawline, feeling the roughness of his skin...

MORE HUCOW BOOKS

SERIES - FAVORITE HUCOWS

1. First Time in the Barn

2. First Time in the Pen

3. First Time in the Shed

4. First Time in the Tractor

5. First Time on the Haystack

SERIES - FERTILE ONLY

1. Bumping the Teacher

2. Bumping the Midwife

3. Bumping the Farmhand

4. Bumping the Sinner

ABOUT THE AUTHOR

Leandra Camilli's obsession? Writing dirty, steamy stories that make her readers drool. She loves her Alpha males, hucows, sissies, and futas. If you're looking for those kinds of books, look no further.

With a cup of coffee on her table and warm socks on, she writes almost every day. Leandra Camilli has featured in several top 100 categories in the store, and she publishes weekly.

www.ingramcontent.com/pod-product-compliance
Lightning Source LLC
Chambersburg PA
CBHW070735160726
48003CB00006BA/2526